THE 10,000 ADVENTURES OF MINNESOTA DAN

Cross-Country Skiing in Mystical St. Yon's Valley

H. R. Maly

Balboa Press books may be ordered through booksellers or by contacting:

Balboa Press
A Division of Hay House
1663 Liberty Drive
Bloomington, IN 47403
www.balboapress.com
1 (877) 407-4847

ISBN: 978-1-4525-9963-2 (sc)
ISBN: 978-1-4525-9964-9 (e)

Library of Congress Control Number: 2014921639

Print information is available on the last page.

Balboa Press rev. date: 7/23/2015

BALBOA.
PRESS
A DIVISION OF HAY HOUSE

The 10,000 Adventures of Minnesota Dan series books

are dedicated to our grand children:

Thais Belle Rulich-Maly

Ava May Maly

Olive Marie Maly

Adelaide Lucille Buonincontro

Stella Thais Buonincontro

Malik Henry Donald Maly

Preface

Daniel Joseph Maly loved to play sports; in particular, swimming and football were his favorites. This true Minnesota kid loved the outdoor life, where he hiked in the hills, built tree forts, would cross-country ski, and camped in the forests. This is the fourth in a series of books that transport young people on a journey that Dan either took or was planning to take before he lost a courageous battle with cancer.

Dan, one of four boys in the household, had fun-filled times with his brothers, Tim, Matt, and Mike. They and Dan's close friends enjoyed his adventurous spirit. Two other significant family members were their golden retrievers. The male, Rusty Bones, and the mom, Miss Megan, were cared for and loved dearly by all the boys. Rusty became Dan's pal, and during the final days of Dan's life, Rusty always stayed near his side.

This last adventure book in the series of four books, is a story about Dan cross-country skiing with his brothers and friends in St. Yon's Valley on the campus of Saint Mary's University. The other adventure books entail Dan's exciting canoeing trip with his golden retriever, a storm-filled sailing experience with his Dad, and his bike trip with his buddy Jay and their encounter with a black bear as they rode through the Amish country in Southern Minnesota. We hope you will enjoy the 10,000 Adventures of Minnesota Dan.

CANADA

Red River of the North

International Falls

UPPER RED LAKE
LOWER RED LAKE

Eagle Mountain

Lake Superior

Lake Itasca

Duluth

Mississippi River

St. Cloud

WISCONSIN

Minnesota River

Minneapolis

W

E

Lake Minnetonka

St. Paul

Mississippi River

MINNESOTA
THE NORTH STAR STATE

In Minnesota, sometimes the snow comes early in the year. Several years ago, right around the Thanksgiving holiday, it snowed a bunch. I mean to tell ya it really, really snowed.

Everyone was amazed at how quickly it accumulated on the ground. Oh sure, it had happened before, but this was a gigantic snowstorm!

The weather prediction announced that at least thirty inches of snow would fall, but I'm here to say we had more like fifty inches!

With schools cancelled for several days and the entire town shut down, there wasn't much to do.

It was Minnesota, after all, and the snowplows were out in full force to clear away the snow from the streets.

Everything was covered by a shimmering mantle of the fluffy white snow, making the entire Hiawatha Valley around the city of Winona look majestic.

Not to worry, though; in Minnesota that meant it was time to go outside and play in the snow.

Several kids in the neighborhood made their way outside and were playing hockey.

So, on to some fun—it was time to frolic in the new snow!

Dan's brothers, Tim, Matt, and Mike, encouraged him to call some of his friends.

With school closed and everything at a standstill around town, Dan called several of his neighborhood friends to see if they wanted to go cross-country skiing.

They whooped and shouted, "Yes, yes!" Someone suggested they use the ski trails at Saint Mary's University, which was not far from where they lived.

Dan's dad agreed and started loading the SUV with the skiing equipment.

At the university, there was a professor who had a passion for cross-country skiing. He also kept the ski trails in great shape.

Many people from town and the surrounding area skied on those trails all winter long.

That's where Dan and his friends decided to ski.

There were always crowds of people waiting to ski at the university.

The ski patrol officer could be seen zooming around on his snowmobile to make sure everyone was safe.

It was easy to make the trip since the university was only a half mile away from their house.

Dan, his brothers, and friends arrived at the university just ahead of a large crowd of people.

The boys took a few minutes to wax their skis.

They did this to prepare to ski the slopes and the beautifully groomed ski trails.

The temperature was a perfect 20 degrees Fahrenheit – a great day to ski.

A really special place they knew of was in nearby St. Yon Valley, back near one of the bluffs along the Mississippi River.

The secluded valley offered all who went there peace and serenity.

The next thing the boys had to do before they began to ski was to become familiar again with their skis.

Putting them on was one thing, but feeling comfortable on them was something altogether different.

Several practice trails were nearby, and the boys were eager to make a few practice runs.

Each helped the other by fitting their ski shoes into the clamps on the skis.

As soon they had everyone fitted out securely, they would be ready to go cross-country skiing.

Heading for the trails of St. Yon's Valley, they felt excited, along with many other people wanting to get on the trails at the same time.

The more experienced skiers moved quickly past them.

Still, a crowd of people clustered at the same place at the same time, trying to climb the hill.

Dan, his brothers, and his friends took their time, though, because they up the first hill and the only way to manage any forward progress was to walk like a duck with your skis on.

On top of the first big hill the boys gazed at the valley in the distance.

They could see several trails leading into the forest.

The skiers now increased the pace, and Dan could see the people spread out along the trail.

Dan and his friends continued skiing in single file and were having great fun as they zoomed up and down some small hills in the valley.

The smooth trails took them into the forest.

With the other skiers ahead, the boys had the forest to themselves. The trails led them up and over a number of small hills again, which became easy to manage.

Then a large hill loomed in front of them and this meant another duck walk to reach the top. Dan made it to the top first and waited for his friends to catch up.

Once all were at the top of the hill, they began their descent, picking up speed like snowballs.

A curve to the right was coming up quickly, so Dan leaned on the outer edge of his left ski, like he was taught, and it pulled him around the curve in fine fashion.

Several of the other boys, however, didn't manage the turn and *ker-plunk* they went, head over skis tumbling into a snow bank.

They laughed about what happened and at how much snow they were covered in, while dusting themselves off.

As Dan stood waiting for his friends to get back on the trail, he noticed a group of six or seven deer in the distance staring at them.

Dan was mesmerized by the scene and at how beautiful the deer looked.

The deer and Dan watched each other.

Dan thought to himself how special it was to see them there in the woods.

He wondered about how God had created so many beautiful, and yet different, creatures in the world.

In a flash he recalled a sermon he had heard, when the priest said that "God is in all things and if you look closely, you will indeed see God in everything."

While his friends and brothers gathered themselves up and began moving down the trail again,

Dan was in awe of the mystical experience of seeing the deer.

Standing there in the forest, he felt peaceful and it became clear to him that God was truly everywhere … if you took the time to notice.

Dan began skiing down the trail to catch up to his friends.

As he approached them, they asked what took him so long.

He laughed and told them he saw some deer and wanted to thank God for letting him see them.

The trail was now winding its way back to the place where they had started this big adventure of skiing the trails in the valley called St. Yon's.

On the ride home, some of the boys talked and some were quiet.

Back at the house, a crackling fire in the living room fireplace brought them welcomed warmth.

Next up was hot chocolate and sandwiches for lunch, topped off by homemade oatmeal-raisin cookies that Dan's mom had made.

Sitting around relaxing and talking about the day, they all agreed that life didn't get much better than what they had experienced.

Gazing into the fire, Dan thought about how lucky he was to know that God was with him, his family and his friends.

Always!

The End

What lessons did Dan learn that day about cross-country skiing?

1. Finding a good safe place to ski is very important.

2. Make sure you check your ski equipment before you set off to go on the slopes.

3. Sometimes it better to practice skiing a few times before you begin your trip on the trails.

4. Try to find places that have good skiing trails already made for you.

5. Make sure that you have the right kind of winter clothing so you keep warm.

6. Mittens are usually better to wear than regular finger gloves. (They keep your hands warmer.)

7. It's fun to go out skiing with your friends.

8. If there are lots of people on the trails be sure you use proper etiquette and be polite.

9. The snowy winter time can be a time of great joy and fun, if you know how to play in it.

10. Enjoy the beauty of nature after all, it is God's creation!

winter gloves

warm ski hat

snow goggles

snow "shoes" for trekking in heavy snow

warm winter jacket and warm pants

special ski pole

special ski shoe bindings

About the Author

Born in New York City, H. R. Maly's career spans over forty years as a teacher, university administrator, and consultant. Currently he is the chairman of Maly Executive Search, a firm specializing in executive level searches and placements for non-profit institutions in both the higher education and healthcare industries. He is a former professional athlete having played in with both the Cincinnati Reds and Minnesota Twins organizations. He served on the board of the North Florida Susan G. Komen Affiliate, and is now an active member of the Ponte Vedra Beach, FL YMCA board of directors. Hank and his wife, Dr. Maggie Cabral-Maly, live in Florida and have five grown children and six grandchildren.

About the Illustrator

After retiring from the Navy in 1977, Charles Immanuel Stratmann taught technical subjects in a vocational school in St. Augustine, Florida. When he retired from that job in 1992, he decided to paint in watercolor full-time. His drawing skills had been honed in the Navy and especially in preparing handouts for his technical classes. He could make complicated systems easier to understand with his illustrations, enhancing what the students could absorb from the textbooks. His drawings and the subsequent watercolors frequently included drawings of people at work or working people at play. Fishing boats loaded with fishermen, parades with marching musicians, New Orleans jazz funerals, and jazz musicians on stage were frequent subjects. He seldom draws from models or photographs. "If I can think of a subject, I can draw it," he says. Charles says a flood of ideas resulted in the sketches incorporated in this story which readers will enjoy. He adds that it was a joy to paint every one of those scenes.

CPSIA information can be obtained at www.ICGtesting.com
Printed in the USA
LVOW02s0149090915

453303LV00006B/8/P